This book belongs to:

....

C E

Published by Reader's Digest Children's Books
Reader's Digest Road, Pleasantville, NY U.S.A. 10570-7000 and
Reader's Digest Children's Publishing Limited,
The Ice House, 124-126 Walcot Street, Bath UK BA1 5BG
Copyright © 2006 Reader's Digest Children's Publishing, Inc.
All rights reserved. Reader's Digest Children's Books is
a trademark and Reader's Digest is a registered trademark of
The Reader's Digest Association, Inc. Manufactured in China.
10 9 8 7 6 5 4 3 2

Are You There, God?

written by Allia Zobel Nolan
illustrated by John Bendall-Brunello

Reader's Digest
Children's Books™

Pleasantville, New York • Montréal, Québec • Bath, United Kingdom

Little Cub heard the wooden floor creak. He peeked out from under the covers, drew them close under his chin, and stared into the darkness. A street light shone through the window and he could see a hairy monster's shadow on the shade.

He was sure another monster just went into his closet, and a third was almost certainly hiding under the bed.

"Are you there, God?" he whispered, then pulled the covers over his head.

Mama Tiger opened the door. "Honey," she asked, "is anything wrong?"

Little Cub sat up. "Monsters are scaring me," he said, "and I can't sleep."

"Little Cub," Mama said. "You don't have to be afraid. God is here and he'll protect you. And if you ask him, he can help you be brave. Okay?"

"Okay," said Little Cub, and he settled down to sleep.

The next morning, Little Cub walked with Mama to the bus. It was his first day of school, and his stomach was doing flip-flops.

"Mama," said Little Cub, "I'm scared."

"Don't worry," said Mama Tiger, as she kissed him. "You'll do just fine." Little Cub got on the bus and looked for a seat. He felt his face turn red.

"Are you there, God?" he said quietly. Then he sat down next to a boy wearing a soccer T-shirt and glasses.

Little Cub didn't know whether he should say something or not. But he figured if the boy was as scared as he was, maybe talking would make them both feel better.

"Nice shirt," he said. "Do you play soccer?"

"No, but I want to someday," the boy said.

"Me, too," said Little Cub. Soon, the two of them were talking nonstop.

Little Cub had made a new friend. His name was Josh.

"Good morning, class," said the teacher, Mrs. O'Mally. "You are very welcome here today. Now, I'd like you all to tell us your name and one thing about you."

Little Cub watched as each boy and girl stood up and spoke. He was surprised at how unafraid

they seemed. Not him. His hands were sweating. His legs felt like jelly. And he could not think of a single thing to say. Then, suddenly, it was his turn.

Are you there, God? he thought silently as he as he got out of his chair.

"I'm Little Cub," he said. "And I...I...." Little Cub swallowed hard and looked at the floor. That's when the idea came to him. "And I've got big feet," he said, and then blurted out, "and...they're great for running fast."

As the boy next to him sprung up, Little Cub sat down. His heart was pounding like a drum. But soon the moment passed, and he felt much better.

"Thanks, God," he said, with a sigh of relief.

At recess, Little Cub found a ball and began kicking it around when his new friend Josh came by.

"Boy, was I shaking in class today," Josh said. "I don't like standing up in front of people."

"Yeah," said Little Cub. "Me, too. But Mama taught me something to remember when I feel that way. She said God can help us be brave if we ask him."

"Can God help us now?" asked Josh nervously, "because I think we're going to need him."

Just then, Little Cub turned and saw a big, scary-looking boy heading straight toward them. He was staring at Little Cub and Josh and he wore the expression of someone who had just bitten into a lemon.

He had two equally scary looking boys alongside him.
They weren't smiling either.

Little Cub's mouth dropped open.

"Are you there, God?"
he asked nervously.

"Hey, Big Feet," said the scary-looking kid. "I'm Charlie, and I heard you say you're fast. Well, I'm the fastest runner around here. Not you," he said.

Little Cub blinked and replied with the first thing that came into his mind. "Well, let's see if you can catch me," he yelled over his shoulder. Then he ran toward the school's entrance.

Little Cub made it there in no time. "Thanks, God," he said.

"Okay, Big Feet," gasped Charlie when he caught up. You really *are* fast. We could use a kid like you on our soccer team. What do you say?"

"What about me?" Josh chimed in.

Before Charlie could answer, Little Cub said, "I don't play unless he plays."

"Well," said Charlie, "okay." Then they all went back inside school.

   Before Little Cub knew it, his first day of school was over.
When the bus came, he sat with his new friends. The five of
them talked soccer until the bus stopped. When Little Cub
saw his mother, he ran to her.

"School was great," he said excitedly. "Wait 'til I tell you." Then, as they walked home, Little Cub told Mama each and every detail of his day.

Bedtime came, and Mama looked in on Little Cub as he knelt to pray. She wanted to ask him how he managed to deal with his first-day jitters so well.

"God," she heard Little Cub say, "Thank you for being there. I was really scared. But it turned out to be the best day ever. Amen."

Mama Tiger smiled and closed the door. She had gotten her answer without even asking.